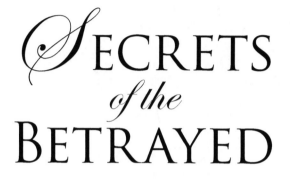

SECRETS
of the
BETRAYED

NATHANIEL HUDSON

authorHOUSE®

AuthorHouse™
1663 Liberty Drive
Bloomington, IN 47403
www.authorhouse.com
Phone: 1 (800) 839-8640

Published by AuthorHouse 04/15/2015

ISBN: 978-1-5049-0539-8 (sc)
ISBN: 978-1-5049-0538-1 (e)

Library of Congress Control Number: 2015905250

Print information available on the last page.

CHAPTER 1

This is amazing; I have friends that support me to the fullest. Sammie thought to himself while sits on his bed and thinks about the camp he and his friends are going to for a couple of weeks, for the bad things they did. While Sammie was sitting in his bed throwing his soccer ball up in the air and catching it again. Trevor, Sammie's friend, burst through the door and Sammie stood up.

"Hey Sammie boy, your mom let me in and told me you were up here," Trevor said.

"So are you ready for boot camp?" Sammie asked.

"Well if it gets me away from my sisters, and plus I don't think we have choice," Trevor said with a grin on his face.

Trevor smiled as Sammie grabbed his bags.

"Hey, why don't you just ride with me and my mom, it will save your mom some time and she's always busy as you know." Trevor said.

"Well, alright, if that makes everyone happy," Sammie said while walking to the door.

They both walked out of the room and down the stairs where Sammie's mom and his little sister Lauryn were sitting at the table waiting to take Sammie to the bus.

"Hey mom, is it alright if Trevor's mom just takes me?" Sammie asked.

"Yes, just call me when you get there," Susan said as she stood up and hugged Sammie.

"Alright, Bye mom, Lauryn," Sammie said as he walked out of the door.

As Sammie and Trevor walked out of the door Sammie saw Emma, who was another friend of both Sammie and Trevor in the car.

"You didn't tell me Emma was riding with us," Sammie shouted with excitement.

"Yeah, I forgot to tell you, I wanted both of my best friends to ride with me," Trevor said.

They got into the car and started driving straight to the bus stop, they didn't want to be late to the bus stop. As soon as they got to the parking lot where they were supposed to meet, the bus wasn't there yet so that's where they sat until the bus arrived. Trevor looked into the rearview mirror and remembered that people used to think that Sammie and Trevor were twins. They both had short brown hair with blue eyes. Emma was more quiet than usual. Emma had brown eyes with short dirty blonde hair but it was enough to put in a ponytail she did so while they were in the car. She had just a little bit of freckles on each side of her cheeks. All three of them have been friends since the first grade, they did almost everything together. Sammie started to get a bad feeling about his boot camp. He had never been there before he heard things about it, but heard that it was a tough camp. The buses finally came after about ten minutes they grabbed their suitcases and bags, and walked toward the bus. Emma started to walk onto the bus; she wasn't paying attention to where she was going and accidentally bumped into another girl that had long brown hair and green eyes.

"Watch it you freak!" The girl said as she pushed her out of the way and walked on the bus.

"What was that about Emma?" Trevor asked while he put his hand out to let her first on the bus. Emma hesitated.

"That's Amber, She doesn't like me or something," Emma answered while she walked to the back of the bus.

Trevor shrugged his shoulders and walked to the back of the bus where Emma was sitting. Sammie followed and sat next to them. The seat was large enough for all three of them. There were four buses full of people and the drivers gave rules to the passengers and then headed to the camp site.

"Emma? Are you really okay?" Trevor asked?

"I'm okay Trevor, thanks, I'm just really tired, I didn't get much sleep," Emma insisted.

The driver said that it would take at least an hour to get to the campsite and it was getting dark so Sammie, Trevor and Emma relaxed and laid back. There was a person on the bus other than the bus driver to make sure everyone stayed on the bus and got to the boot camp like they were ordered to.

"Did you know that girl who you bumped into earlier?" Sammie asked Emma

"Who Amber not really," Emma said.

"She looked like she had a lot of hate toward you. She looked really mean," Sammie said.

"Well the last time we met we had some troubles."

"Troubles, Troubles like what?" Sammie asked.

"Ask me when we get to the camp I'm tired," Emma said closing her eyes.

The buses finally arrived at the boot camp site at around 7:30 pm, everyone were really tired. There were camp directors there to show them where their assigned cabins were. There were two boy dorms and two girl dorms. Sammie and Trevor were assigned to the same boy's dorm, Number one. Emma was assigned to girl dorm two, which was just a block from each other. There were about 23 boys in the dorm room with Sammie and Trevor. Each boy was given a card that showed them which bed was theirs.

They had to sleep on bunk beds. Sammie and Trevor's bunk was towards the back where there was a back door on the far side of the bed. Each camper had to follow the same dress code as they could see from seeing the campers that were already there before them. They were wearing black shirts, black pants, and black boots. All the boys were standing with their bags in front of the dorm. The dorm watcher Mr. Butcher stood in front of them.

"He looks really mean," Trevor said to Sammie.

After he said that Mr. Butcher started to talk.

"I need everyone to shut up and listen, I have two rules, do what you're told and read the handbook that is on your beds. Now, let's get to it," Mr. Butcher walked away.

When he was done talking he over to his desk in the middle of the room. Everybody walked to their assigned bunks, and each found a trunk by their beds that they were supposed to put their things in and they had their uniforms neatly folded on their beds. After Sammie put his stuff in his trunk he opened his handbook and started to read it, so did Trevor and most of the dorm.

We have to sign in every morning and every night or else we will get a written warning and have to mop the floor. Trevor thought to himself with a questioning look on his face.

"Well at least we get three meals a day," Trevor said while shrugging his shoulders.

"Well this is going to be fun," Sammie said.

"I guess so," Trevor said.

There is a six hour work day for the campers, which is basically work out and discussion classes, and on the weekends there are usually activities unless someone messes it up for everyone which usually happens. Sammie threw his hand book on his bed and started standing up, Sammie and another boy that had curly red hair, and a little bit taller than him stood up at the same time and bumped into each other.

"Sorry about that," Sammie said.

"It's okay," The boy said.

"Hey, what's your name?" Sammie asked.

"Will, what's yours?"

"Sammie, What did you do to get put in here you don't look like a bad kid at all?" Sammie asked will while leaning against his bunk.

"Ugh, it's a long story we go expelled from school," Will said while kind of rolling his eyes.

"Wow, For what?" Sammie asked as he sat down on his bed while facing will.

"My friends and I tried to prank the principle but it didn't end good," Will said.

Will knew he just made that up, but he had to make up something, he had been here before and found out that nobody really cares why you're in here anyway were all just trying to get in and get out of here as soon as they can.

"We were court ordered to come here," Will said sitting on his bed facing Sammie.

"We were planning on getting out of here sooner than later," Will said kind of rolling his eye's

"You just got here," pointed out Sammie.

"I've been here before and it's horrible," Will said.

"It can't be that bad, all you have to do is listen to what they say and you'll do just fine," Sammie said.

"That's what they want you to think Sammie, you have to realize how things are in the world, how it's full of crazy people." Will snapped.

Sammie looked at him like he was crazy.

"Sorry about that, I get a little excited sometimes, so are you in or not?" Will whispered.

"I'll talk to Trevor about it," Sammie then stood up as the dorm watcher ordered everyone to go to the cafeteria for dinner.

The cafeteria was about two blocks from the dorms. Once Trevor and Sammie got to the cafeteria they saw Emma sitting at a table by herself. They went over and sat by her.

"Are you not going to eat?" Trevor asked Emma.

"No, I'm not hungry," Emma said.

"Well I am getting in line," Trevor said.

Trevor walked into the line and Sammie and Emma stayed at the table.

"Hey, I was talking to a boy named Will in my dorm, and he was talking about getting away from this place," Sammie said while looking at Emma.

Emma didn't hesitate at all.

"Well let's do it!" she said.

"What?" Sammie questioned.

"I don't want to be here either, I mean all you do here is workout, go to counseling and have people you don't even know telling you what to do all day, at least that's what they say and I don't want to do that," Emma said.

"We are here for a reason you know, and we are in the middle of nowhere," Sammie said.

"We will figure something out, we have to keep quiet about it though," Sammie said.

Trevor came back to the table with his tray of food. Emma glanced over at Trevor and then looked back at Sammie.

"Does he at least know about this?" Emma asked Sammie.

"Know about what?" Trevor asked while taking a bite out of a French fry.

"About getting out of this place," Sammie said.

"Yeah, I overheard you and what's-his-name, Will, talking about it, I think it's ridiculous since we're in the middle of nowhere, We wouldn't even have a chance of surviving out there, wherever you're planning on going," Trevor said.

"There are going to be quite a few of us and we can take whatever we need," Sammie said.

"You guys are going crazy," Trevor said

"So when are we leaving? "Emma asked.

"As soon as," Sammie trailed off.

Just then Will and his friends Amber and Joe sat at their table. Trevor and Will looked at each other in a strange way and then quickly looked away. As Amber sat down she started to think again why she doesn't like Emma. Amber doesn't like Emma because she is jealous of Emma. Emma doesn't like Amber because she acts like a spoiled brat.

"Have you talked to Trevor about it?" Will asked Sammie while nudging him.

"I don't know about Trevor but Emma is on board," Sammie answered while looking at Trevor.

"Okay, okay I'm in but I'm not doing anything crazy," Trevor announced.

"You're in here because you did something crazy, "Joe pointed out.

"So when are we leaving?" Amber asked again, but this time looking at Will.

"I am thinking tomorrow night," Answered Will.

"That's too soon! "Joe said. Everyone looked at him.

"We just got here, and we need to keep this quiet because if anybody hears about this then we are screwed until the end of this program," Joe said in the most strong and convincing voice he had.

"Well it has to be soon, we can't let the watchers know what we are up to, so we can't go too early but we can't stay here either," Amber said to Joe.

"I think the day after tomorrow will work perfect," Joe said.

"I think that will be perfect," Amber agreed.

"Then let's do it," Concluded Will.

They all then ate their food, at least those who had any, and then went to their dorms when they were finished and shut down for the night.

CHAPTER 2

By the time the day came for their escape plan to go into action they had figured out where they were going to go. Wills' grandpa used to own the land and he had shelter still standing out in the woods. It was a few miles out but they were going to be able to walk to it. The plan was for them to leave just before lights out. They had already stashed away necessities that they had stolen from the cafeteria to survive off of that should last them for a while.

Will, Joe, Trevor, and Sammie headed towards their bunk beds.

"I really hope you guys are ready," Will said as he grabbed his bag.

They were all splitting up and meeting at the start of the woods. When Sammie was looking around he noticed the small door by the side of his and Trevor's' beds.

"Come on guys, I see a little side door over here, let's go now," Sammie whispered.

The boys all started to move towards the door in the most inconspicuous way possible. When they got close enough and the watcher changed his attention they made it to the door and attempted to open it, only to find that the door was jammed, but with their combined efforts they all got the door open while still drawing no attention to themselves.

Sammie, Will, and Trevor all got out but while Joe was getting out he saw another camper see him so he walked back to the watcher. The rest all ran toward the start of the woods. When they got there they saw Amber and Emma already there waiting. The boys were all out of breath and when Joe got there and started talking Sammie cut him off and started to talk.

"Are you guys ready?" Sammie said.

"Yeah let's go," Emma answered.

They all started walking into the woods, moving branches out of the way, swatting at bugs, stepping over big rocks trying not to trip or fall. While they were on their way, Joe completely forgot to tell everyone what he saw at the camp.

"How far is this place?" Joe asked while sitting on a very hard, unsmooth, and uncomfortable rock.

"Come on Joe!" Will reprimanded.

"We don't have time to rest!"

"Let him rest Will we have all been walking for a long time," Amber said in a slightly loud voice.

"Shut up Amber no one was talking to you!" Will said in an even louder voice.

"You know what Will, you have been acting weird lately," Amber said.

"No I have not," Will said with a strong attitude.

"Hey! We do not have time to argue, we have to stay focused," Emma said

"Yeah, Emma's right, we have to work as a team if we want to get through this, we were lucky to get this far but to really get away we can't argue over this stuff," Sammie added.

"Look guys, we really have to go," Emma said to them.

"Who made your boss? "Amber questioned.

"I'm not trying to be the boss, I'm just saying that we should get going," Emma defended.

"You think you're the perfect little angel but you're not, you being in this camp with the rest of us are just proof of that" Amber said.

"Shut up Amber you have been jealous of me since we met!" Emma accused.

Before Amber could respond footsteps from a distance were heard. Everyone immediately fell silent and started running towards into the woods. After what seemed like a lifetime of running Sammie saw the shelter.

"Hey look there it is Hurry!" Sammie yelled.

They ran as fast as they could to the shelter. When they got there the door was locked.

They checked the back door but it was locked too. Emma tried a side window and was able to crack it open, but it was jammed so she couldn't open it any further. Emma called for Sammie to help her. When Sammie got there he was able to get the window to pop open and immediately helped Emma in.

"Hey guys, over here," Sammie called to the rest.

Sammie then helped Amber, Joe, Will and Trevor in. One by one everyone went in. When Sammie was in he re-shut the window. They were all so tired and out of breath. When they looked at each other they all sighed with a huge sigh of relief. Emma got up and tried a light switch.

"Hey Will, do you know where the fuse box is?" Emma questioned.

"I don't even know if this place has one," said Will.

"There has to be one," Emma demanded.

"There are light switches I'll go outside and try to find it," Emma said.

"No!" Will yelled.

Emma looked at him with a startled face.

"I mean, Trevor and I will go and try to find it," Will said.

At that, Will and Trevor went towards the door while everyone else sat on the floor in a circle with their two flashlights that they borrowed from the camp. Trevor and Will tried to open the door but it was jammed from this side as well. Eventually they got it open by using enough force. They closed the front door and looked back to make sure no one was listening.

"So the plan is still on?" Trevor questioned.

"Yeah so don't mess it up we are doing well so far, just be careful about talking about it with the others around," Will advised.

"I don't think there's a power box out here." Trevor said.

"There isn't there isn't any electricity in this shelter at all, I just needed to make sure you have the plan down," Will responded just as Emma rounded the corner.

"Hey guys did you find it?" Emma asked.

"No, I don't think there is one," said Will.

"Well come on, let's get back inside," Emma said while starting to walk back towards the front of the shelter. Trevor and Will followed Emma back to the house and then all of them sat down on the floor next to everyone else.

"So who do you think was following us back there?" Amber asked.

"I don't know, maybe it was just a deer or something," Sammie said.

As soon as Sammie said that Joe remembered that he was supposed to tell them that another camper saw them escape. He didn't say anything though because he was afraid of how they would react to that information or to him for keeping it from them for so long.

"We should look around this place and see what's here we are in the middle of nowhere we never know who or what could be here," Joe offered.

"Joe is right, I'll go look upstairs," Emma Offered.

"I'll go with her," Sammie said.

Emma and Sammie went to the stairway next to the kitchen. It was really dark and they couldn't see anything. The floor made weird noises when they walked over it. Emma and Sammie started to walk up the stairs. The stairs were extremely unstable but both made it up them safely. They both started to check the rooms and closets.

"Sammie, I have a feeling that something is wrong with this whole situation," Emma implied.

"What do you mean?" Sammie asked.

"Like with Will, he is really secretive and controlling," Emma said.

"I feel like that too, but it's probably nothing, don't worry about it," reassured Sammie.

Sammie walked to the window that was across the room and just stared out of the window into the darkness of the woods.

"So who do you really think there was someone chasing us back there in the woods?" Emma asked.

"I don't know, it could've been anyone or anything," Sammie said.

"Do you promise we will get through whatever this is together?" Emma asked hesitantly and quietly while extending her pinky finger towards Sammie. Sammie Smiled and wrapped his pinky finger around hers. "I promise," Sammie said as they both walked back down stairs.

CHAPTER 3

Everyone sat down on the couch that they found in the living room. They all sat there in silence just trying to think.

"So, since we're all here, why don't we all say why we were put in boot camp instead of just staring at the walls," Will suggested with a great bit of attitude.

"Why don't you go first since you want to bring it up?" Emma suggested.

"You guys should know," He said.

Amber stood up quickly and looked at Emma.

"What are you talking about?" Amber asked.

As soon as Amber said that Will pulled out a gun that he had retrieved from his grandfather's hiding spot and pointed it at Amber.

"Everybody sit down and shut up!" Will yelled.

Trevor walked slowly towards Will.

"Calm down Will," Trevor said trying to get him calm down a little.

"I thought we were in this together," Will said.

"Wait, you guys are in this together?" Emma questioned.

"Yes we sure are," Trevor confirmed.

"I knew there was something weird going on!" Emma said.

"It wasn't what it looked like just put the gun down and i'll explain!" Amber yelled.

Everyone looked at Amber in a weird way.

"What are you talking about Amber?" Emma questioned.

Before anyone could say anything else someone ran up from behind Will and tackled him to the ground and the gun flew out of Wills' hand. Trevor grabbed the person off of Will and threw him against the wall.

"What are you thinking, who are you?" Trevor yelled at the kid as Will got up.

"My name is Josh and we need to leave now," He said.

"Why did you tackle me?" Will asked.

"You had a gun in your hands!" Josh yelled.

"Thanks Josh, he was about to shoot me in the head," Amber said.

"We need to leave now," Josh demanded.

"How did you find us and what are you talking about?" Emma asked looking at Josh in a confused way.

"I saw you guys leaving the dorm, so I followed you, but when I was leaving the Watchers saw me and started running after me, I think I lost them but I'm not sure, which is why we have to leave now." Josh informed.

"Why would you follow us we could of gotten away, where are we going to go now, they are probably following us!" Amber yelled.

"I know that there's this island called Willow that we could go to, "Josh offered as Emma looked at him in a weird way.

"But we are going to have to move fast if people are following us," Josh said.

"I don't know who to trust anymore," Emma said while looking pointedly at Will.

Will just looked at Emma and went to the window and then looked out of it.

"So how far is the island?" Emma asked.

"Its, maybe a couple of miles from here," Josh replied.

"My grandpa has owned this shelter for a long time and I've never heard anything about any Willow Island," Will said.

"Well you can stay here because I'm not going to stay here and get caught," Emma said.

"Me too, are you in Joe?" Amber questioned.

"Yeah sure, I'm in," Joe confirmed.

"The walk gives you guys time to explain yourselves if you're going to come, but know that I have both eyes on you," Emma told Trevor and Will.

"We should leave now, I saw something move out there in the woods," Josh said as they all rushed out the back door and started following Josh.

Everyone naturally started to walk in a line of sorts. Sammie and Emma were in the back of the line.

"I knew something was up with those two," Emma admitted.

"I should of known, what are we going to do about them, I don't know if I can trust any of them anymore," Sammie said.

"I don't know but we are going to have to keep a close watch," Emma informed him.

As they were walking Joe was thinking that things were too quiet so he went over and started to talk to Amber.

"Hey Amber," Joe said.

"What do you want Joe?" Amber asked impatiently.

"I've been meaning to tell you something but I never got to it," Joe nervously said.

"What do you mean?" Amber asked curiously.

"Like back in the camp when Trevor, Will and I were leaving I saw Josh, or I think it was Josh who saw us leave and walk towards one of the watchers," Joe explained in a hushed voice.

"Are you serious, are you sure it was Josh?" Amber asked.

"Not really, but I really think it was him, but you know that gun Will had?" Joe asked.

"Yeah what about it," Amber inquired.

"When we were leaving the shelter I grabbed it," Joe said as he looked at everyone else to make sure they weren't listening.

"Oh, well keep it hidden Joe, just in case we need it but let's keep this between us okay," Amber Whispered.

"Okay, I will," Joe said.

Chapter 4

Everybody walked slowly through the woods still trying to get to the island. Sammie tapped Emma on the shoulder.

"Hey Emma," Sammie said.

"Yes Sammie," Emma said while looking back at Sammie.

"You said, you said you had problems with Amber in the past," Sammie reminded her.

"Well let's just say she is really stuck up and doesn't think of anyone but herself, but you want to know who the real problem is," Emma asked.

"Trevor and will," Sammie finished.

"You got it," Emma said

Before either of them could say anything else Josh interrupted.

"Hey guys, what were you thinking when you were planning on doing when you got to the shelter?" Josh asked.

"We were going to stay there until we figured something out or until the camp was over," Sammie said.

"How far is this island from where we are now," Trevor asked.

"It's not too far from where we are now," Josh responded.

"You're not off the hook Trevor," Amber said.

"Shut up Amber," Trevor said harshly.

"Stop it you guys," Sammie reprimanded.

"What are you talking about they were planning on killing us," Amber passionately objected.

"Wait, where is the gun?" Will asked.

Amber and Joe looked at each other but no one said anything.

"Come on Trevor, give it up," Emma demanded.

"I swear i don't have it," Trevor protested.

Before anyone could say anything else, Josh started yelling.

"There is Willows Island!" Josh yelled with excitement.

"Where is it?" Emma asked.

"Over there right across the river, let's stop talking and start walking," Josh said as the moon reflected off the water.

They all started rushing towards the river with their flashlight.

"How deep do you think it is?" Trevor asked.

Sammie grabbed a branch that was about six feet long and stuck it in the water and it went in about five feet.

"Okay we can walk across but it's really cold," Sammie said.

"I can't swim," Amber said.

"You don't have to swim dummy you just have to walk," Will said in anger.

Amber didn't reply to Wills comment and stepped into the river and started walking, everyone followed behind her, and it was about 15 feet to the other side. When everyone made it across they were freezing cold.

"We can't keep going like this," Emma said.

"We have to if we don't want the watchers to find us, were in big trouble already, not to mention that we were in trouble the second we got to the boot camp," Josh snapped.

"Well if it weren't for you guy's i wouldn't be here in the first place,"

Trevor said in anger.

"Trevor, we need to get dry before we get sick," Amber said trying to get him to calm down.

"Wait I Want to know what happened," Josh said.

"We don't have time for that right now," Emma said.

While Josh and Emma were arguing, Joe looks across the river and see's lights light there were people holding flashlight or something.

"Hey guys," Joe said trying to get everyone attention but nobody paid any attention.

"Hey Guys!" Joe yelled as everyone looked at him.

"Just shut up and look across the river!" Joe yelled as they all looked across the river.

"Are those the watchers?" Amber asked.

"Just get down," Joe said.

"No we need to run," Amber said.

"They would hear us running," Joe said.

"We need to stop arguing, and do something, they are getting closer," Emma said.

"Where did they go?" Amber asked with a confused look on her face.

"Turn that flashlight off!" Emma yells.

Everybody gets to the ground and tries to blend into the darkness. The watchers blended into the darkness it seemed.

"I think we should run," suggests Amber in a frightened voice.

"Be quiet Amber," everyone reprimands at the same time.

After about five minutes of waiting in the bushes alongside the river, everyone got up and looked to the other side of the river to see if they could determine if the watchers were on the other side.

"I don't see anyone, I think they're gone," Josh said with certainty

"I think we should go now," Sammie said.

As soon as they turn around, two watchers were standing behind them.

"Well, well, look what we have here, bunch of little trouble makers," Watcher number one said.

"I hope each of you read the rule book," Watcher number two said.

"No one cares about the stupid rule book," Amber said defiantly.

"Ask your friend here," Watcher number one said.

"Who would that be?" Amber asked.

"That would be me," Josh said.

"What but we trusted you," Amber yelled.

"That was the point Amber!" Josh yelled.

"Why would you do this to us you're in this place just like the rest of us," Amber says.

"See, that's where you're wrong let me explain, I'm undercover, I do this only summer to make sure kids like you don't escape," Josh explains.

"Well what are you going to do; take us back to camp and call our parents?" Trevor asked.

"No, we're going to keep you right here on Willow Island," Watcher number two answers.

Were just going to have a little fun while we can watcher number two thought to himself knowing he was supposed to just bring them back to the campsite.

"What, what are you keeping us here for?" Emma asks.

Amber and Joe were off to the back of the group to start talking.

"There are more of us then them," Amber said.

"Yeah, you're right, and we still have the gun," Joe agrees.

"What are you planning on doing with it? "Amber asked.

"I don't know yet, I'll figure something out," answers Joe.

Amber was hoping he didn't do anything crazy, she was hoping that he would just scare them away, but she didn't really put much thought into it.

CHAPTER 5

They weren't supposed to be doing this to them, they were supposed to be bringing them back as soon as they found them, but Josh convinced the watcher's to have just a little bit of fun with the power that they did have at this boot camp. Watcher number one was in the front of the group and watcher number two was in the back. No one in the group really knew what was going on. Nobody had escaped and made it this far from the bootcamp before. They walked for about half an hour they came upon a site that had benches and a table and three big lanterns that lit up the whole site.

"What is this? Amber asks with a very bad attitude.

"Okay now i need everybody to shut up and sit down everybody," Josh demands with a strong voice.

Each watcher stood on either side of the group like they were bodyguards. Sammie and Emma sat next to each other and

Amber and Joe sat next to each other, so Will and Trevor sat next to each other. Josh was in front of them all.

"Everyone is here for a reason, since you guys want to escape how about we discuss what all of you did here and now," Josh suggests.

No one said anything, It was a dead silence.

"So no one wants to go first." Josh says

"I will," Amber says.

Emma looks at Amber in a strange way.

"You don't have to do this, you don't have to talk," Emma insists

"I think it's best if I say this." Amber says.

"Yeah, I think it is best if you just say it," Agrees Trevor.

"What are you guys talking about?" Sammie asked.

"Just let me explain!" Amber screamed.

"The reason that most of you guys are in here is because of the day when we were in the woods, when we were found with a homeless that was beat him up really bad," Amber explains in a deeply saddened voice.

"Yeah I remember that day that's basically the reason why I'm here," Joe says.

"I'm sorry Will," Amber cries.

"Wait what are you being sorry for we didn't do it," Joe said as he looked at amber in a strange way.

It all happened on a sunny day. Emma and Trevor were hanging out in the woods and they saw this man in the woods. They had no idea that the man wasn't homeless, much less that he was Will's' father. They started throwing rocks, poles and bricks at him that they found just in the woods. Once they knocked him over they ran away as fast as they could, not knowing that they had hurt him very badly. They ran into an abandoned road with a dead end where they met Joe and Amber. Amber immediately didn't like Emma for some odd reason, but that was just how amber was back at the time she was just that type of person. Amber started calling Emma names for no reason; stupid, ugly, funny looking. Emma just thought she was a spoiled brat, but Emma didn't say anything back she was the person to try to ignore that kind of negative behavior so Emma just looked at her in a disgusted way. Joe told Amber to leave her alone and just keep going. Trevor and Emma walked out of the woods as Joe and Amber walked into the woods. Amber and Joe walked through the woods, moving branches and all of a sudden Joe trips over a body and Amber trips after him. They both look at each other. Police officers run towards them without knowing the people from the area had reported suspicious activity going on in the woods. Amber and Joe tried to explain to them that they didn't do this to him, but who listens to teenagers, no one believed them. Will's dad was taken to the hospital, they didn't know what exactly happened to him after that, Will didn't want them to know Amber told Trevor while they were in the boot camp that they're the ones that almost killed will's dad in the woods and the Trevor remembered what happened that day and realized that he and Emma did do it and felt bad but didn't want to take the blame so he convinced Will that everyone else had something to do with it except him that's why Will and Trevor did what they did inside the shelter. They were taken into custody and found guilty and then sentenced 20 hours of community service and had to take counseling because of their age or else worst things could have happened to them. Before they did that, they had to go to boot camp. When Will found out he was furious he and his mom got into a huge argument over it, not knowing his mom had been drinking, his mom was telling him how his dad was a deadbeat and was no good. Will then pushed her down the stairs out of anger and broke her neck and back, she went to the hospital and Will was sent to the boot camp and counseling sessions. Will was in the camp the before because of trouble with his mother.

Emma and Trevor were in the boot camp for trespassing and vandalism. Everyone looked at Will in a sympathetic way.

"You told me you had nothing to do with it Trevor," Will said looking at Trevor with lots of anger.

Trevor didn't say anything at all, he really didn't know it was will's father but when will was telling him the story about what happened to his dad, right away he knew it.

"So you were lying about the teacher thing all along?" Sammie asked as he looked at will in a strange way.

"Well yeah, nobody tells the truth about being in that boot camp," said Will.

"You're all little liars," Josh said.

No one minded what josh even said

"Sorry, we didn't know," Emma and Trevor said at the same time said.

"I thought you were on my side Trevor You can't apologize now," Will said in anger as he Will starts to charge towards Trevor.

Sammie grabs him and tells him to calm down. Will turns toward Amber.

"I thought we were friends Amber!" Will yells.

"What did we do, we just found him there badly hurt, the police just thought that we did it they're the ones who did that to him," Amber said.

"You knew his whole time and didn't tell me, were supposed to be friends!" Will yells.

"I said I was sorry," Amber cries.

Joe sat there in silence while trying to think of a plan to escape.

"Okay, I've had enough, you're all going back to camp," Josh says.

"Wait, you're taking us back?" Joe asked.

"Now you guys get to deal with Mr. Butcher and the rest of the camp leaders," Josh informs them with no remorse.

"I'm not going," Joe said with a straight face.

Everyone looked at Joe.

"We're already busted; we might as well go back. Amber said.

"I said I'm not going I'm sick and tired of being treated like crap all the time so no matter what anyone says I'm not going back, I'm staying right here on Willow Island," Joe said in an unmovable voice.

The watchers and Josh all looked at Joe.

"Joe, we are only going to tell you one more time to get up and go one more time or else," Josh warns in a strong voice.

Joe reached into his pants and pulled out the gun and pointed it directly at Josh.

"Or else what?" Joe asks.

Josh didn't say anything.

"That's what I thought, ever since I first met you I knew there was something wrong about you, you look our age but you're really not. How's that even possible huh, do you wake up every morning and put on makeup or what How old are you really?" Joe asked in anger.

He walked closer to Josh.

"I'm the same age as you I just do this because I have to," Josh answered.

"Just put the gun away, we're already in enough trouble already!" Emma yells.

"Be quiet Emma!" Joe yells.

"Listen to your friend Joe, just put it down," Josh said.

Josh starts to walk towards Joe.

"Take another step and I'll blow you away," Joe warns.

"I saw you see us when we left, I knew you were onto us,"

As soon as he said that Watcher number one charged towards him. Joe shot him in the chest and fell instantly. Then he shot Josh in the head and the other watcher in the leg and chest. Everyone started yelling and screaming.

"What did you do Joe?" Amber cries.

"Joe stop put the gun down!" Emma yells.

Joe dropped the gun.

"What were you thinking Joe?" Trevor yells.

"It's over now, it's been over since we left camp, we have to keep going," Joe said.

"So you're telling us you knew Josh was a fake from the start and you didn't tell us?" Emma asked in anger.

"No, I didn't know at all," Joe said.

"But you said you saw him see us leave," Amber pointed out.

"Hey, if you think about it, I'm not the only bad guy here, Joe said.

Nobody says anything to that. Will looked at everyone and everyone looked at him.

"We're sorry Will, we didn't try to hurt him that bad, it was supposed to be a prank," Emma said.

"It's okay guys, I forgive you It's was in the past now we have to stick together now," Will said in a calm voice.

"How can we stick together if we keep secrets from each other?" Emma questions.

"Let's just keep going, we're going to be here for a while, we all have to promise not to keep secrets from each other anymore," Will says.

They all agreed and promised not to keep secrets from each other. They looked back at the dead bodies, picked up their flashlights and walked in the other direction. They all thought about their families but they didn't care anymore at this point. They decided there was no turning back from what they did.

They knew that they were going to be on Willow Island for a while. Sammie thought his mom and sister and started to tear up, but wiped it away before anyone could see it. They had been out there all night and were tired. They found a place deeper in the wood far away from the bodies where they could all lay down and rest for the night. It took a while for them fall asleep in the woods especially on the ground. They made little pallets out of dead leaves, it was the best they could do at the time. It was so silent all they could hear were the crickets in the background but all they could think of is what just happened. It was dead silence but after a while everyone just fell asleep, Sammie was still up. as he laid his head on a bed of leaves and started into the darkness, he stayed up for the most part of the night just thinking.

CHAPTER 6

It was sunrise and the way that Sammie was positioned the sun hit him right in the face and woke him up instantly. Sammie looked around and everyone was still sleeping. They were exhausted from the long horrible night. Sammie thought long and hard, he was the only one that didn't tell his story of why he got into the boot camp last night and hoped that nobody asked. He thought about the time he and Emma promised to stick together no matter what. He wondered if there were any other camp directors that were looking for them since the others one won't show back up. Then he thought about his mom and his sister Lauryn and how much he missed them, and wondered if they were thinking about him or even knew that he escaped and they were looking for him. Sammie stood up and as soon as he stood up Emma jumped up in terror.

"Oh my, Sammie you scared me!" Emma yelled at Sammie.

Emma started kicking everyone telling them to get up. Everyone stood up and looked at each other.

"Well are you guy's ready for this or what?" Sammie asked while looking at everyone. They all shook their heads yes, they all stood up and started walking deeper into the island.

"How big do you think this island is?" Amber asked.

"We wouldn't know Amber, we haven't been out here before," Sammie said.

Amber didn't say anything. As they walked further into the island they started to see fewer trees like they have been cut down.

"What do you think happened here?" Sammie asked.

"I have no idea," said Will.

Joe stopped all of a sudden, and then everybody stopped.

"Do you guys realize what we are doing?" Joe asked in anger.

"Calm down Joe, we will figure this out," Emma said in an attempt to calm him down.

"How are we supposed to survive out here, we have little food and little water, you guys are crazy!" Joe yelled.

Everyone looked at each other and thought that he was right. How were they going to survive out here in the middle of the Willow island. They all have family at home waiting for them. They were in trouble either way though Sammie. They had killed people out here, they can't go back or else they would all be put in jail. Amber started to tear up.

"We're not going to make it, Joe is right, we have to go back or we're all going to die out here," Trevor said.

"I'm going back you guys, have fun out here!" Joe yelled as he started walking away.

As soon as he started walking he was hit by a rock and he fell over. Everyone freaked out. They didn't know where it had come from and they all ducked down toward the ground and Will yelled out to see who it was, but nobody answered. Joe stood back up rubbing his head where the rock hit him.

"Who are you?" A boy yelled out.

He stood where no one could see him.

"Come out," Amber demanded.

From behind the bushes a boy showed himself. He looked about thirteen or fourteen with long curly hair. "I'm 14," The boy said

He had clothes on that we're really dirty and ripped. He also had dirt on his face like he hadn't bathed for months. he looked really scared.

"What's your name?" Emma asked.

"Greg," He answered.

"How long have you been here, are you by yourself?" Emma asked.

He didn't say anything, he just looked at Sammie and Sammie just looked at him. Greg didn't take his eyes off of Sammie for a while. Then he looked back at Emma.

"I don't remember, it's been a long time," Greg said.

"Are you here by yourself?" Emma asked.

"Now I am, everyone else that was here either," Greg stopped talking.

"Everyone else did what Greg?" Emma demanded.

"They either died of sickness or committed suicide because what they did was so horrible that they didn't want to go back or even live," Greg said with sadness in his voice.

Everyone was silent for a moment.

"So Greg, why are you still here, and where are you staying?" Sammie asked.

"I don't care what happens, I'm not going back," Greg said with certainty.

Before anyone could ask him what he was talking about.

"So Greg, can you show us where you stay?" Emma asked.

"Sure," Greg answered.

"I'm still leaving I'm not going with you guys," Joe said.

"We'll leave then nobody cares anymore!" Amber yelled.

Joe looked at Trevor and Will.

"Are you coming with me or not?" Joe asked Trevor and will.

"I feel like I don't have chance of surviving out here so I'm going," Trevor said.

Yeah me too," Will said.

"Okay then," Joe said.

Joe, Trevor, and Will all walked away.

Suddenly Emma yelled to Will.

"Wait Will!"

Will turned around and looked at Emma.

"When you told me it was your dad that we almost killed, there aren't any words that can explain how much sadness and guilt I felt and how sorry I am," Emma said with tears in her eyes.

Will walked up to Emma and gave her a hug.

"It's okay Emma, there's nothing we can do about it now it's in the past," Will said.

Will and Joe and Trevor walked back into the wilderness on the way back towards camp. It was just Amber, Sammie, Emma, and Greg left. They had no idea what they were getting into next, but they knew they were not going back to that camp.

"Well I guess I'll show you guys were I'm settled," Greg said while walking away.

They all followed him in silence as they walked to a place with no trees, sort of like a camp site. There was a little shelter that Greg built, but not big enough for all of them to fit in. Emma was wondering what he did with the bodies of all his friends that died and decided to ask.

"So what did you do with the bodies of those who died?" Emma asked.

Greg answered by pointing at an area with dirt obviously dug up and then replaced over the bodies. No one said anything after that.

"We have to survive," Amber said.

"Are we really just planning on staying here, we need to think of something!" Sammie yelled.

Greg looked at Sammie, but Sammie noticed that Greg was looking at Emma too. Emma noticed how the two looked at each other from time to they met.

"So Greg, how did you end up in this out here?" Emma asked.

Greg just looked at Emma and then looked at Sammie, and then back to Emma. But before he could say anything Sammie cut him off.

"Shut up Greg and come over here!" Sammie yelled as they both walked away from everyone else.

Everyone was stunned.

"Everyone thought you died Greg, but you're alive and that's great, but don't say anything about what happened." Sammie demanded.

Everyone was looking at them with wonder when they looked back.

"They're going to find out eventually, we should just tell them now," Greg said.

The story behind Sammie and Greg is that they are half-brothers they had the same dad and Greg lived with them when there mom and dad were married. They haven't seen each other for two years. Their mom sent him to live there dad when they got divorced when they were little because Greg was a so called trouble child. The reason Sammie is in there is because Greg lied on their dad and said he beat him. Greg would hurt himself to make bruises and would say their dad did it. So there dad is in prison now. Sammie attacked him with no mercy and was sent to a mental hospital and was declared as mentally impaired so eight months later he was sent to the camp because they found out later that he had nothing wrong with him. Sammie was out of the hospital for two days before he was sent to the camp and he never told anyone the truth about it. Greg was one years old when there dad met their mom, one year later Sammie came, a couple of years after that here came Lauryn. While Sammie was in the hospital, Sammie and his mom told everyone that he was going to a private school. Sammie never told Emma or anyone of his friends that he had a brother.

"So this whole time you were lying to us, how could you do that?" Emma asked while wiping her tears away from her eyes.

Sammie just looked at everyone for a while, he didn't want to say anything at all, but he thought it was about time he should start telling the truth about everything and stop keeping secrets from his best friend. Sammie looked back at Emma.

"I didn't want you guys to think I was actually crazy when I'm really not I just had a moment I'm sorry Greg I'm sorry Emma I'm sorry everyone," Sammie said quietly.

"Sammie, I'm like your best friend, we grew up together how you could think that, you can tell me anything, but you chose to lie," Emma said.

This conversation wasn't about surviving or trying to figure out what they're going to do. Amber, Trevor, and Greg went inside the shelter that Greg built and sat there and looked at each other without saying a word, they didn't know what they were going to do at this point.

"What else is there Sammie?" Emma asked.

"That's all I kept from you Emma, I have a little brother, I was never in that private school what else do you want from me?" Sammie asked.

Emma turned around and kicked a rock and screamed as loud as she could.

"Sammie we made a promise, but you know what Sammie, we have more things to worry about now, let's just stop keeping secrets and figure out what we're going to do there going to find us, we have to get off this island or figure out something quick," Emma said.

"I don't want to go back there," Sammie said.

"We are definitely not going back there we just have to go somewhere else other than here there going to find us, even though Greg has been here for this long but I think we might of blew his cover, we need to go," Emma said.

"No matter what happens, I'm leaving this place in the morning, even if I have to stay up all night to figure out a plan," Emma said.

They all had a bad feeling that staying on this island was going to cause more problems they all heard what happened to Greg's friends; they didn't want that to happen at all. They all sat down It was getting dark, Greg started a fire in the pit that he made. While Sammie was sitting in silence he thought about his mom and sister, he was wondering if they knew that he had escaped from the boot camp. Amber turned away from everyone. amber lived with her mother, they didn't get along at all and didn't even care if her mother was worried or not, all she knew is that shedidn't want to stay with her, all she wanted is to stay with her grandmother until she graduated. Even though Amber knew Joe she really didn't know his story well no one did. Joe was the type of guy to keep things to himself, so no one bothers asking him. Greg had some rabbit meat that he caught earlier that day that he cooked and shared it with everybody. They haven't eaten at all day. They all separated on the camp, they were sick of each other and it wasn't even night fall yet. they just sat there all day just thinking about what has happened to them already. Time went by so fast, the sun wasn't even set yet but they all chose to go to sleep early. They laid there on mats made out of leaves. Most of them didn't even go to sleep right away they just laid there until they could.

CHAPTER 7

Emma was up before everyone they had all slept through most of the day, she was just sitting there thinking about where they all were going to go. Sammie woke up; he started stretching it was a long night for them. He looked at Emma.

"Hey Emma what's going on, why are you up so early," Sammie said as he propped himself up facing Emma.

"I was just thinking," Emma said.

Sammie just looked at her and thought about all the stuff he told her last night. Emma was his best friend and apparently his only friend. Trevor betrayed him well they all did. Sammie looked back at Emma.

"Sammie, I really have to tell you something," Emma said in a really sad voice.

Sammie didn't say anything he just looked at her a listened.

"You know how I was staying with my dad and all?" Emma asked. while looking at the ground.

"Yes of course I have been to you house plenty of times," Sammie said with kind of a smile on his face as he remembers those days.

"Well that's not my dad, I just said it was, he is just an old family friend that felt bad for me, and I don't even stay with him," Emma said with tears running down her face.

"Wait what, we had movie nights and everything there," Sammie said in anger.

"Well it was all a lie Sammie I stayed in an orphanage Sammie an orphanage," Emma repeated while crying into her hands.

When Emma was born her mother died soon after. Her father disappeared when she was just three years old. She has been in the orphanage since then, that's where she met Greg, When Greg stopped living with Sammie and his mom and sister and went to live with their dad there dad was sent to prison he was put up for adoption. A couple of months after he was adopted his adoptive parents were in a car crash and they died so Greg was sent to this orphanage where Emma was staying then he ran away to live in the woods, everyone really thought he died or something.

"That's the story he told me okay Sammie I don't mean to tell his story like that but that what happened I promised him I would never tell but I felt you needed to know that," Emma said.

"It's okay Emma I know that it's not your fault, I never knew that about either of you, but now we just have to figure out how to get out of here," Sammie said while looking down at Greg.

"No Sammie were staying," Emma yelled.

Sammie looked at her in confusion

"Wait what are you talking about," Sammie yelled.

After he did that everyone woke up.

"What going on," Amber said while rubbing his eyes.

"We're leaving this area," Emma said.

Amber looked at her like she was crazy. Amber had no idea what happened between those two while they were sleeping but he had a bad feeling about what happened.

"Well where are we going?" Amber asked.

"Anywhere but here," Sammie said as he looked at Emma.

"Wait Sammie we're not leaving the island, you didn't let me finish what I was saying!" She yelled to Sammie.

Sammie didn't say anything he just glared at Emma.

"We made a promise remember, to stick together no matter what," Sammie said.

Amber looked at them. When did they make that promise he thought to himself. Emma walked up to Sammie.

"You're right we did make a promise, that's why you have to trust me," Emma said.

Amber cut them off before they could say anything else.

"Wait where are we going exactly," Amber asked while looking at Emma.

Emma looked at amber and didn't say anything then she looked away and started thinking about the house she used to pass every day when she used to sneak away from the orphanage. It was such a big house and she never seen anybody come in out of the house. All the windows were boarded up and stuff. It seemed scary so she never attempted to go in until now. Emma looked back at amber.

"Hello I asked you a question," Amber said while waving her hand trying to get her attention.

"We're going to that house," Emma said.

Greg looked at her in a strange way because he knew exactly what house she was talking about but he didn't say anything about it because he thought no one knew he stayed at the orphanage and plus he wanted to get out of this area and do something other than sit out here in the middle of know where.

"Greg you can stop lying about everything now, she told me," Sammie said as he turned away from Greg.

Greg already knew what he was talking about and looked at Emma. Emma winked at Greg.

"Where is the house," Sammie asked.

Emma started walking everyone shrugged their shoulders and agreed to go to the house and started to follow Emma. Amber wanted to clean up a little bit before they went so they all went over to where Greg had buckets of water from the river and cleaned up. They started walking so they could get there before dark. They all walked in a straight line. After they had been walking for a while amber started complaining about her feet.

"Are we almost there I'm getting tired," Amber said.

"We're almost there amber," Emma said just trying to get her to be quiet.

The house was about another half a mile and it took them about an hour to get through the woods. Once they saw the driveway they started running until they got to the middle of the driveway. Everyone except Greg walked up to the porch and stood by the front door trying to figure out how they were going to get in. Greg just stood in the driveway looking into the only window that wasn't covered up by a board. He looked up there in a nervous way knowing that there was something bad about this idea but he wasn't sure that all that stuff he heard about this house was true so he decided to kept it to himself. Greg walked up to the porch with the others. somebody painted on the board that was nailed to the door to keep it shut. It said do not enter in big bold words, but they didn't care what it said. the house was boarded up and old look as if no one has been in there for centuries. Sammie went around to the side of the house to see if he could find anything to get that wood of the door so they could get in. He found a shed that was connected to the house. He went to open the little screen door and it just came right open. He went in there and he found a tool box, and in the toolbox was a crow bar. He took the crow bar back up to the front and told everyone to stand back. He it into the side of the wood and the crow bar slipped out, so he tried it again and with hardly and force the bored popped right off.

"Well there it is," Sammie said while looking at Emma.

Sammie just looked at Emma in a strange way.

"Why are you looking at me like that Sammie?" Emma Asked.

"I Don't know," Sammie said.

"Snap out of it Sammie," Emma said as the door creaked open.

They all just shook it off and walked in the house as the floors creaked. They all started coughing because the house was so old and dusty. They were in the living room and there was still furniture in there. there was even a TV and it was plugged in. It looked like people actually lived there. As they all stood there in shock Sammie decided to go into the kitchen. He started looking around. There was a island in the middle of the kitchen with pot and pans hanging from above. He started opening up the cabinets and there was actually staple foods in them. Emma walked into the kitchen. She opened up the fridge; there was milk eggs and everything.

"Do you think somebody still lives here?" Emma asked in a nervous way while looking at Sammie.

"I really hope not but it really looks like it, let's go look around some more," Sammie said.

They walked back into the livingroom where amber and Greg just stood there.

Emma didn't expect it to be like this at all but there was food water and furniture so far so good, if only they were the only ones there. They all stayed together and walked up the stairs, there were spots on the walls like there had been pictures there but they took them down, as soon as they got to the top of the stairs there was a long dark hallway they didn't see a light switch but to the left there was a window at the toward the middle of the hallway it was almost sunset so they could still see where they were going as they started walking down the hallway where they approached a door. They all looked at each other as Sammie put his hand on the door knob and started to open it and then they all heard a noise coming from down stairs.

"Did you guys hear that," Emma whispered.

Everyone nodded their heads yes.

"You guys stay here, I'll go see what it was," Emma said.

"No we are going with you Emma, were in this together," Sammie said.

"I'm not staying up here by myself," Amber said.

Everyone looked at her then they slowly walked down the stairs. Once they reached the bottom of the stairs, they just looked around to see if there was anybody or anything there. Then a woman yelled.

"Hey what are you guys doing in here, this is private property!" she yelled.

Everyone turned toward the voice. She was standing in the kitchen on the other side of the island. She walks to the entrance of the living room. It was an older lady with red hair and glasses. Sammie started to stutter.

"We just got curious to what was in this house," Sammie said just trying to make something up.

"Ewe," Amber whispered as she stared she stared at the lady.

Everyone looked back at her and told her to shut up.

"You kids have no right to just walk in my house," the lady said as they all looked back at her Were so sorry we will leave right now." Emma said as she turned around to walk out the door.

"No wait," the lady said.

They all turned back around.

"Charlie Sarah, come over here, we have visitors," the lady said.

They stood there in silence as the lady pointed at Sammie.

"You come," The lady said.

Sammie walked toward her. He she looked him in the eye.

"My name is Carrie, I live with some others and they cannot be out there with other people," Carrie explained.

"What is she talking about Sammie," Amber asked.

Sammie looked back at Amber.

"I have no idea," Sammie said.

Sammie looked back at Carrie as she got in his face, Sammie jumped back.

"I know you," Carrie said.

"Wait hold on, I don't think you have the right person because I don't know you," Sammie explained.

"Yes I do your adopted, your one of a kind I can pick you out of a whole field of boys your age," Carrie explained.

Sammie looked at her in confusion.

"Im sorry Carrie we really think that you have the wrong person," Emma said while grabbing Sammie.

"No I'm the one who gave you away I would know, I was your foster mom when you were a baby, your mom's name is Susan right?" Carrie asked.

Sammie didn't say anything he just looked at her in confusion. He couldn't believe what he was hearing his mom wouldn't do that to him, or maybe she would. Then he thought about it he didn't even look like any of his family. Sammie didn't say anything after that he just stood there in disbelief. Emma looked at Carrie.

"You said there were others?" Emma asked as Charlie was standing right behind Carrie nodding his head no, but Emma didn't think anything of if it.

"Well there down stairs in the basement playing, do you want to meet them," Carrie asked.

Emma thought that was sort of odd but she went with it. Emma looked back at Amber, Greg and Sammie they all said they wanted to meet them.

"Well follow me there right this way," Carrie said.

She led them to the kitchen where there was a string that opened up a door from the floor. Greg thought about saying something about the house. The stuff he heard about this house was really true he knew Carrie was out of her mind. This house wasn't the house she claims it to be, he struggled to say something but before he could get anything out Carrie opened the door from the floor.

"Well here it is, let's go," Carrie said a she put her hand out pointing down the stairs. Emma went first she knew this was a bad idea from the start but she just thought about these poor kids in this basement, one plays in a basement like this well at least she didn't. She lead the way as everyone followed. Carrie was behind everyone and once they got to the bottom of the stairs there was a hallway leading to a room of light. They started walking down the hallway and they noticed that the walls were made out of sharp pieces of rock and bricks, but they just kept following the glow of light down further into the basement. Emma looked behind her and noticed that Carrie was farther away back then everyone else but she just kept walking, she wanted to see what these other kids are up to. They reached the end of the hallway and they didn't believe what they saw. There wasn't a soul in the room; there were just six beds in there three on one side and three on the other side with lanterns above the beds that were so dim they could barely see anything. This is what Charlie wanted to tell them. Charlie, Sarah and four others were kept down here. They all turned around and Carries face was really red, they were all frightened by it.

"You're all terrible children and you deserve to be locked up!" She yelled as she started running back down the hallway.

Emma wasn't happy about that at all and she didn't think about anything else she just knew she was going to be locked up down here. Emma ran after Carrie at full speed, as they she got closer and closer they both met at the stairs. Carrie started running up the stairs, Emma grabbed her by the feet and Carrie fell. Everyone caught up to them.

"Go!" Emma yelled.

Everyone rushed past them as they wrestled, everyone made it out to the top of the stairs, and they looked back down.

"Come on Emma!" Sammie yelled.

Carrie was on top of Emma trying to get to the top, that's when Emma kicked her down the stairs. She tumbled all the way down to the bottom of the stairs. Emma got up slowly and looked down at Carrie motionless body at the end of the stairs not knows if she was alive or not.

"Emma come on hurry up, we have to go!" Sammie yelled.

Emma walked up the stairs and they closed and locked the basement door.

CHAPTER 8

It has all come together now, the others were the ones that were once out there with Greg, those are the ones that got away, those are the one who couldn't take it anymore those are the one that didn't make it. They all just realized what they just did, that's why they have to get off this island, everyone that ever thought Greg, Charlie and Sarah were dead can now know that there alive. The truth is Carrie is an evil person, she kept kids locked up down there in the basement and abused them, and treated them like they were slaves. She could never have kids of her own so she started doing foster care and after a while she started making up lies saying that they ran away and never came back, but really brought them right here to this house she owned on Willows Island. She turned a love toward children to a strong hatred towards them, but now that all comes to an end. One thing they do know is that Charlie and Sarah we in so much shock that they just stayed quiet. Nobody blames them after all the stuff they went through.

"I don't think we should stay after all of this, I think we should go back, each and every one of us," Amber said strongly.

"Yeah I think Amber is right, that's the best thing we should do at this point no one has to ever know about this," Sammie said looking at everyone. Emma backed up from everyone with such a confused face.

"What are you guys thinking, we can't just leave here and act like nothing ever happened on this island, I just kicked a lady down the stairs not knowing if she is alive or not!" Emma yelled as she turned and hit the wall.

"What's up with you Emma, we can't just stay here I'm pretty sure they're out there looking for us now, we all have someone out there who cares about us," Sammie said.

"Says the boy who actually has a family, my parents died, nobody is looking for me," Emma said.

Sammie had a loss for words for a while until he remembered.

"I'm sorry Emma, but we made a promise remember, we will always stick together no matter what, we can't survive out here Emma, you heard what happened to those other kids," Sammie yelled.

Emma didn't say a word.

"Emma maybe my mom can't adopt you like she adopted me," Sammie said.

"Sammie I'm sorry but I'm not going," She said quietly as she backed up.

"What?" Sammie asked.

"I said I'm not going, I'm staying right here, I have everything I need you don't have to worry about me ever again, just leave right now!" Emma yelled.

"Let's just go Sammie she is doesn't want to come with us," Greg said.

Sammie looked at Greg, in confusion.

"What are we going to do," Sammie yelled.

"I'm taking Charlie and Sarah back to town, I don't care what happens to me at this point," Greg said.

Sammie looked at Emma but didn't say anything; they just looked at each other.

"Are you going to be alright Emma?" Sammie asked.

"I've been through too much already to not be alright, what makes you think I can't handle being out here, just leave Sammie i'll be just fine, maybe we will see each other again someday, I'm starting over I have no one else, I just have my self now this has been private property for a long time, no one is going to come in here looking for anything," Emma said while having a little bit of a smile on her face.

They all started walking out the door, but Sammie just stood there looking at Emma. Greg pulled Sammie as he almost fell.

"Are you coming?" "Greg asked as they walked toward the front door.

They didn't even know if Carrie was dead or not, it was almost like they forgot what just happened. They didn't care; Emma just made the decision of her life just now. They all went out the front door and didn't even look back it was dark outside. They didn't know what time it was and they didn't know how they were getting back to town but they started walking. They knew they were going to get off this island if it was the only thing they were going to do. They walked in the dark for hours with the little flashlight they took from the campsite. They approached beginning of the island at the river where the body of the watchers and Josh laid. They just stood there and looked at them in shock; they still couldn't believe what Joe had done. Amber had tears in her eye. Charlie and Sarah were frightened; they hadn't seen a dead body before. Actually none of them have until that day.

"Who are they, and what happened how did they get here?" Greg asked as Amber and Sammie looked at each other.

"You don't want to know," Sammie said.

They all held on to each other and they walked across the river. They got really wet and dirty, but they didn't care they just wanted to leave. There was a highway, the road they took to get here, they were planning on getting to that road and following that road all the way back to town, but they needed to get past the boot camp. They can't get caught going back to the boot camp, or who know what could happen from there. They would rather go back to town and deal with it. Sammie was silent most of the way there, they all were but Sammie was in so much shock that Emma decided to stay there. They got to the end of the wood where they saw the boot camp.

"What are we going to do?" Amber asked.

"I'm not going back there," Sammie said.

"We can just crawl all the way to back to the highway without anyone seeing us," Greg insisted.

They sat in the woods where no one could see them until it was dark enough for them to leave which seemed like forever to them.

"Well let's go, I am so ready to get out of here," Amber said while raising her eyebrows.

"We have to be careful, the watchers obviously know that we're gone there on the lookout for us once we get to the highway we have to run fast at least until were out of the site of the boot camp," Sammie said.

They started crawling; they went as fast as they could without making as much noise as possible. They made it to the highway without being seen, they reached a ditch so they had to climb up and out of there to get onto the highway. Once they did so they stood up and started running, there are street lights so they didn't have to use the flashlight anymore so they just dropped them and kept running. They didn't have much energy because they haven't eaten much, so they stopped running; they were able to see the boot camp any more. So they just stopped right on the side of the road there were no people no car no anything just plain old road. They stood there with their hands on their knees catching their breath. Once they caught their breath the all just looked at each other.

"Hey guys I know I, know I haven't been the nicest person before all of this happened, I have been so mean to everyone, especially Emma and I just wanted to say I'm sorry," Amber said.

"It's okay Amber, you don't have to apologize to anyone, we all have been through a lot, and what just changed the lives of all of us, what going to happen to us I don't know but we are probably going to regret it but we can't change the past but I just found out that I was adopted and I wouldn't have found that out if we didn't do what we did, I just want to get out of here and get home just like you do," Sammie said.

Before anyone could say anything else Greg started yelling.

"Look, headlights!" Greg yelled. as he pointed toward the lights.

Everyone looked then they started yelling and waving at the car hoping that it would stop. The car eventually stopped, it was a light blue van that pulled up, a woman and a man jumped out of car.

"Are you kids ok?" The women asked.

They all nodded their heads yes.

"Come on get in its chilly out here," The man said.

They all stepped into the van and sat there in silence. The women and the man looked back at them.

"Where are you kids headed?" The man in the driver seat asked.

"We are headed into town, the same direction you guys were already going," Sammie said.

"What were you kids doing out here by yourselves?" The women asked as the man started driving into town.

Amber and Sammie both looked at each other as they try to make up something to say. "Umm, we were looking for our dog and we got kind of lost," Greg said.

"Way out here in the middle of nowhere, that's kind of odd," the lady said as she turned back toward the road.

"We loved that dog, we had ever since I could remember," Greg said while looking at amber and Sammie shrugging his shoulders.

"Well I'm glad we drove by here and seen you kids," the lady said.

It went silent after that, as they drove into town the sun started to rise as there was mist in the air. They didn't think about what was going to happen to them they just wanted to get home.

CHAPTER 9

As they drove into town they sat there in silence just thinking. Sammie thought about Trevor, Will, and Joe and what happened to them when they came back. He wondered if they even made it back. Then he thought about these poor kids Charlie and Sarah, they were so mentally damage they didn't even talk. They finally made it back into town; they pulled into a empty parking lot.

"Where do kids live, do you want us to take you to your houses?" The lady asked while she looked back at them.

"No, no thank you, we can walk from here," Sammie said as he opened the door.

"Are you sure," She said to be certain.

"Yes, were sure," Sammie said as they all stepped out of the car.

"Thank you for giving us a ride back," Amber said as they all waved goodbye.

The women are her husband drove away without looking back. As the car disappeared the all look at each other in wonder.

"So, what do we do now?" Sammie asked.

"Well I'm going to my grandmother's house, I don't know what you're everybody else's plans are but this might be the last time I see you guys, I really hope it's not but if is, I hope you guys will be okay and all," Amber said as she started walking away.

Then Sammie ran up to Amber and hugged her.

"I know we didn't even know each other before all of this happened and I know you and Emma had problems in the past but I just wanted to say I wish the best for you and I hope everything works out with your grandmother," Sammie said.

Amber didn't say anything she just hugged him back and walked away as she waved goodbye to everybody. Sammie walked back to where everyone else were standing. He looked at Greg.

"So what are you going to do at this point, everyone thinks you guys are dead or something," Sammie said.

"Well, I'm taking them to the police department, as you can tell there really traumatized, and I don't know what I'm going to do," Greg said as he shrugged his shoulders.

"Greg, I'm sorry for everything," Sammie said.

"It's Okay We are brothers, stuff happens, Greg said as they walked in different directions as they waived by to each other.

Sammie walked all the way home, he was so tired, they didn't get any sleep. He walked up to his front door, and stood there for a while thinking about if he should even think about bringing up the adoption or not, but he just rang the doorbell, and his mom answered. Susan opened the door and she saw him standing there, they didn't say anything at all. Susan just looked at him in shock. Then she grabbed him and hugged him as hard as she could. They both walked into the house, as she pulled Sammie into the house she looked behind him to see if anybody was here with him. She didn't see anyone at all. Susan looked at Sammie.

"Sammie where have you been, we've been searching all over for you we couldn't find you anywhere!" Susan yelled as she woke Lauryn up and she came down stairs and stood at the staircase just watching them talk.

"Mom that's not even close to being important right now," Sammie insisted.

"What are you talking about, you escaped the boot camp we thought you were out there dead or something, why couldn't you just finished your time and come back home!" Susan yelled.

Sammie totally ignored the question.

"Why didn't you just tell me," Sammie asked.

"What in the world are you talking about Sammie?" Susan asked as she shook her head.

"Why didn't you tell me I was adopted, why did I have to find out this way, she told me mom," Sammie said.

Susan looked at Sammie in confusion.

"Who told you?" Susan asked calmly.

"Carrie told me, and did you know that Greg is alive?" Sammie asked.

Susan was speechless because she knew exactly what he was talking about, but she couldn't believe it, he disappeared a long time ago.

Lauryn walked into the living room.

"Am I adopted too mom?" Lauryn asked as she looked at the ground and sat down on the couch.

"I'm sorry that you had to find out this way but I didn't want you to know because you have already been through enough and I thought that it would best if you didn't know at all, and yes Lauryn you're adopted to," Susan said as Sammie cut her off.

"It's okay mom I forgive you," Sammie said while looking at his mom.

"You know there looking for you right Sammie," Susan said.

Sammie didn't say anything, he knew what he had to do he just wanted some sleep before it all happened. He went to his room to take a nap because he knew that today he had to turn himself in. He didn't want to hide he wanted to do this so that's what he did. As soon as he woke up from his nap, Susan went to turn Sammie in, even though she didn't want to, but she knew she had to. The judge sent him to an all-boys maximum security facility for a year in a half to two years. There was a built in school so he would have to attend school there. It wasn't jail but it sure felt like it to Sammie there were no hand cuffs or cells, just lots of force and strict rules. Will went to stay with his aunt and had no contact with his mother due to what happened, the judge put him in therapy classes and gave him community service. Nobody knew where Greg went after he dropped Charlie and Sarah off at the police station, he just disappeared again no one has heard from him since. Amber was let free because they found out the truth about what really happened in the woods that day, she had nothing to do with will's dads beating, or prank as Emma and Trevor called it. Amber got what she wanted; she went to stay with her grandmother's until she graduates. Trevor went back home with his parents and sister, like it usually was before all this happened but he had to go to counseling and was not allowed to leave the house unless he was in school or at counseling for up to six months for what he did to will's dad. Joe was sent to a juvenile detention center for the crimes that he did. He told them where the bodies were but they were sorry for that, I really hope that you accept that, but there is more that I have been hiding from you, all that stuff I told you about the orphanage is all true but I know you're wondering how I was getting to and from the island, how food and water got to the island, is Carrie is alive or not, but anyways besides all that, I have to tell you a secret."

Before she said anything else the phone made a scratching noise and then hung up. "Emma!" Sammie said yelling at the phone.

TO BE CONTINUED.........

Printed in the United States
By Bookmasters